# Rumination

Written by: Jesse Betea

## Chapter 1 - People

A young schoolboy sits silently in his chair, the kids around him are all playing around.

The children noticed his distance and began to berate him, he didn't do anything about it, but he thought in his mind about why these people berate him, he didn't really listen to what they were saying, only affected because of the beration, he only made up reasons why they were berating him.

Boy— You're an idiot, Your worthless, Your ugly, You piece of shit.

The young boy, now 16, sits silently in his chair, as highschool students, the other children are grown as well, as he looks around in his chair, he notices some from the past, and new faces of those he met, who have also met him as well.

Similarly, the other students sit silently in their chairs, as they all listen to the teacher, while she lectures about algebraic equations, she takes a moment to look around the classroom as well, and she takes notice of the boy, and notices he isn't paying attention.

Teacher— "Misugi, pay attention!"

The boy, named Misugi darts his attention towards the teacher and nods his head in a manor to imply respect, Misugi, who is now paying attention isn't actually all there towards paying attention, he hears the girl sitting behind him snicker, and he begins to sweat, but he feels cold.

Misugi— How could she laugh? She thinks I'm stupid? I just wasn't listening, now everyone thinks I'm an idiot, God I'm an idiot.

**** Earlier ****

The girl, sitting behind him, named Sarasa, sat in her chair silently.

As she was listening to her teacher in class, she noticed the boy sitting in front of her looking around.

Sarasa— What's he looking for? And what was his name? Masu- no, Moosa- no—- Teacher— "Misugi, pay

attention!"

Sarasa— Ooh, Misugi, but imagine Moosagi, *Snickers*

*Ring!!!!*

As the bell rang for lunchtime some students began to leave the classroom, others stayed in the classroom and began to

socialize together.

As Misugi began to leave the classroom he couldn't help but think of the girl who laughed and looked back at where she sat and unknowingly, he rudely glared at her.

As Sarasa was sitting in her chair, she thought of Misugi and looked back at where he was leaving, she naturally had a smile on her face, so naturally she smiled at him.

Simultaneously they locked eyes, on one end, a face of welcome, and on another, a face of contempt, both faces misunderstood by the two.

## Chapter 2 - Connection

Misugi— Why is she looking at me? Is she laughing at me again? I'm not stupid, why does she think im stupid?

Sarasa— Why is he glaring at me? Did I do something wrong? No, maybe he's just tired.

Misugi looks back at the door and heads towards the catering area at his school, hoping to forget what happened and forget the 'hateful' girl, unbeknownst to him, Sarasa decides to follow him.

As Misugi nears the catering area, he feels someone grab his shoulder and hears them call out to him.

Sarasa— "Misugi, how are you? You seem tired."

Misugi— Huh? Why is she asking me that, is she trying to demean me more?

Misugi— "What? Why do you care, why, do you want to laugh at me some more?"

Sarasa— "Huh? Why would I laugh at you? I'm only asking how you feel, you seemed tired in class."

Misugi— "Uh, I'm sorry for jumping to conclusions like that… but I'm fine, thank you for asking, I'm sorry, again, what's your name? I'm sorry I don't really remember it."

Sarasa— "No need to say sorry, my name is Sarasa, you are Misugi right? And I should be sorry, why do you think I was gonna laugh at you?"

Misugi— "No reason, I guess. I am Misugi, nice to meet you, Sarasa"

Sarasa— "No reason? Huuuh? You gotta tell me, we're friends now, right?"

Misugi— "I do? We're friends?"

Sarasa— "Of course we are, we shared our names, didn't we? So, tell me!"

## Chapter 3 - Names

Misugi— As a child I had never given a thought towards my name, it's just my name, right? It wasn't a crest to wear or a title to live as, it's just my name, right? But names do have a meaning, for example part of my name refers to the station in one's life, the other refers to error, even though names don't have much semblance, I'm always weary of the error I may cause and I only make sure I don't cause any error, i'm too scared of what would happen if error arises, i'll always make sure I do it right.

He had never thought a bond could be shared just between a shared knowledge, but that is itself a connection, even

two names between people can bring them together.

# Chapter 4 - Self

Misugi— Should I tell her?

Would she be mad if I thought of her like that? No, I should tell her, she would be mad if I lied to her.

Misugi— "I'm sorry, when the teacher scolded me, you laughed, and I thought you were laughing because I might've acted stupid. So I thought you were going to call me stupid when you walked up to me."

Sarasa— "That sounds stupid, I would never think you were stupid I don't know much about you, I'll have to admit that I did see you not paying attention, but I only laughed because I forgot your name, and thought it was Moosagi, funny name right? But atleast I remember it now because the teacher said the real one!"

Misugi— Huh? She isn't mad? At least I told her the truth, but that is a funny name.

Misugi— "Haha, that is a funny name, again I'm sorry that I thought of you like that."

Sarasa— "No need to say sorry, you didn't break my back or anything."

Sarasa smiles at Misugi as she says this.And at that moment, Misugi felt himself.

## Chapter 5 - Somewhere

Sarasa— "Wanna go somewhere after school?"

Misugi— "Uhh, sure, but where?"

Sarasa— "I don't know, anywhere, walk to the beach or look under the bridge, we can walk anywhere, can't we?"

*Ring!!!!*

Sarasa— "Oh, that's the bell, see you later, let's meet at the gate after school!"

Misugi— "Ok, see you later!" Misugi and Sarasa both head to their respective classes, waiting to meet each other after school.

Student--- Man i'm soo bored, this class makes me want to fall asleep.

As the student looks around, he notices Misugi sitting next to him and decides to talk to him.

Student— "Yo man, what's your name?"

Misugi— "Huh me? My name's Misugi, what's your's?"

Misugi— Who is he? Why is he talking to me? I didn't do anything.

Ensei— "Nice meetin you Misugi, my name's Ensei, ain't this history class boring?"

Misugi— "Uhh, yeah this class is a little boring"

Actually, Misugi finds this class interesting, he's fascinated by history and how things came to be, but he wouldn't tell Ensei, he'd be weird for liking something that much, especially a subject widely viewed as 'boring', he doesn't want to be boring.

Ensei— "Yeah, I can't remember a damn thing because teach keeps rambling on about mesotolamia or whatever."

Misugi— "You mean Mesopotamia? *Snickers*"

Ensei— "Hey don't laugh, I just forgot the name that's all!" Teacher— "You two! Stop talking and pay attention!"

Misugi and Ensei both apologize and continue listening as before.

Misugi— Shit, shit, shit, not again, now this class thinks I'm stupid as well, Ensei is probably mad at me for getting us in trouble as well, God I'm so stupid.

Ensei— *Snickers*

Misugi— Huh, maybe it's not that big of a deal, he doesn't seem mad.

Misugi finds joy in this moment, and unbeknownst to him he begins to snicker as well.

Both Misugi and Ensei begin to laugh out loud, interrupting the class, but Misugi doesn't care; as he's found another connection through the shared joy between himself and Ensei.

Chapter 6 - Later

**** After class ****

Misugi sits in his last class of the day, just an hour until he meets Sarasa after school. He's excited to meet someone new, but it feels like time is ticking slower as he waits for the class to end.

Misugi— When is this class going to end? Maybe Ensui's right, these classes are boring, I wonder where we're going to walk? I can't believe Sarasa and I are already friends with just a name.

*Ring!!!!*

Misugi— Oh, the class is already over, must've felt long with me talking in my head.

Misugi walks outside the classroom and heads to his locker to grab his stuff, after grabbing his stuff he heads to the front gate to meet Sarasa.

Misugi— What am I gonna talk to her about? I can't think of anything to ask about, or anything to even say, I'm kind of nervous now.

Sarasa— I can't wait to meet Misugi and

hang out with him,

I'm so excited to have a friend!


Misugi arrives at the front gate and makes

eye contact with Sarasa, being nervous he

darts his eyes away.


Misugi— No, I shouldn't look excited to see

her, that'd be weird, wait, we are friends,

right?


Although nervous, Misugi shifts his eyes

towards Sarasa's again and in a moment of

thought he decides to greet her, for once without worry.

Misugi— "Hey Sarasa, it's nice to see you again! How's it going?"

This greeting from Misugi brings joy towards Sarasa, seeing as it felt true, instead of an obligatory greeting from any well-mannered person.

Sarasa— "Nice to see you too! I'm doing great, how are you?"

Misugi— "I'm fine, thank you for asking."

Although Misugi was doing great, he felt joy from the interactions he had that day, but to him it feels too mushy to say that, she doesn't need to hear how he feels.

Misugi's response confused Sarasa, since the contrast between his greeting and his reply was far apart.

Sarasa— "Just fine huh? Are you sure? You seemed more than happy back there, are you too embarrassed to say it? Remember? I wouldn't be laughing at you!"

These words made Misugi think for a moment.

Misugi— Why have I been acting like people are gonna berate me? Yeah I acted stupid that time in class, but no one called me stupid, and Sarasa wasn't even laughing at me then, and she hasn't even been mad or rude once because of me, is it really that big of a deal, maybe i'm not so stupid, yeah, maybe thinking like that is stupid.

Misugi— "Yeah, fine sounds stupid, sorry, I'm happy to see you, Sarasa!"

Sarasa— "Sounds right!"

# Glossary

Mushy - Overly Sentimental

Misugi - English spelling for a japanese word, with each

individual part, called kanji, represents one's station in life, and the other representing error.

Sarasa - English Spelling for calico, the texture calico, there was no though towards this name

Ensui - English spelling for salt water, which in his name's context, is using to represent him as carefree and adventurous, like an adventure in the salty seas

## Author's Writing

I put a lot of thought into some of the names based on the characters. Look out for the next volume soon, thank you for reading!